Tiny Goat in Trouble

The Royal Society for the Prevention of Cruelty to Animals is the UK's largest animal charity. They rescue, look after and rehome hundreds of thousands of animals each year in England and Wales. They also offer advice on caring for all animals and campaign to change laws that will protect them. Their work relies on your support, and buying this book helps them save animals' lives.

www.rspca.org.uk

Tiny Goat in Trouble

By Mary Kelly
Illustrated by Jon Davis

■ SCHOLASTIC

First published in the UK in 2014 by Scholastic Children's Books
An imprint of Scholastic Ltd
Euston House, 24 Eversholt Street
London, NW1 1DB, UK
Registered office: Westfield Road, Southam, Warwickshire, CV47 0RA
SCHOLASTIC and associated logos are trademarks
and/or registered trademarks of Scholastic Inc.

Text copyright © RSPCA, 2014
Illustration copyright © RSPCA, 2014

ISBN 978 1407 13967 8

RSPCA name and logo are trademarks of RSPCA
used by Scholastic Ltd under license from RSPCA Trading Ltd.
Scholastic will donate a minimum amount to the RSPCA from every
book sold. Such amount shall be paid to RSPCA Trading Limited
which pays all its taxable profits to the RSPCA. Registered
in England and Wales Charity No. 219099
www.rspca.org.uk

A CIP catalogue record for this book is available
from the British Library.

Printed and bound by CPI Group (UK) Ltd, Croydon, CR0 4YY
Papers used by Scholastic Children's Books are made
from wood grown in sustainable forests.

5 7 9 10 8 6

This is a work of fiction. Names, characters, places,
incidents and dialogues are products of the author's imagination
or are used fictitiously. Any resemblance to actual people,
living or dead, events or locales is entirely coincidental.

www.scholastic.co.uk

1

Harry woke to the sound of cockerels crowing. For a moment, he couldn't think where he was. They didn't have chickens at home. . . Then with a grin, he remembered. He was staying on Aunt Judy and Uncle Martin's farm while his mum waited for the new baby to come. With a whoop of excitement, Harry pulled on his clothes, jumped out of bed and ran down the stairs. There was nothing he liked more than helping out on the farm, and to make things even better, it was the school holidays. That meant he'd get to spend all day with the animals.

"Morning!" he called, as he burst into the kitchen. As usual, it looked warm and welcoming in a messy, topsy-turvy kind of way. The post lay in an untidy heap on the kitchen table, cookery books fought for space on the window sill and Patch, Aunt Judy's spaniel, was lying stretched out against the warmth of the cooker. Harry bent down to scratch his tummy. A moment later he felt something bump against his leg and looked down to see Tilly, the West Highland terrier, demanding some attention.

"You're up early," said Aunt Judy, coming over to give him a quick hug. She was dressed in mud-spattered jeans and a jumper and her wavy brown hair

was fluffed up around her face, as if it had been fighting with the wind.

"I didn't want to miss anything," said Harry. He'd come to help out on the farm before, but it was his first time actually staying the night, and he knew work started early. "Am I in time to feed the chickens?" he asked.

"I've left them for you," said Aunt Judy, "but you'd better do them before breakfast. Strut the cockerel is definitely saying it's feeding time." As she spoke, the cockerel let out another ear-splitting crow. Harry and Aunt Judy grinned at each other.

"I'll get my wellies," said Harry, rushing towards the cloakroom. Patch left his warm space by the cooker and padded along at his heels, hopeful of another tummy scratch.

"Patch! You need to stay here," said Aunt Judy, calling Patch back towards the kitchen.

"Can't he come with us?" asked Harry.

"A duck has just started nesting by the pond," said Aunt Judy. "I don't want Patch scaring her away until she's settled."

"That's so exciting," said Harry. "Then we'll have wild ducklings along with all the other animals."

Aunt Judy laughed. "It's not as if we're running short of animals to look after."

Harry had to agree. Aunt Judy and Uncle Martin kept a herd of dairy cows, a coop full of chickens, a large tabby cat, two black-spotted pigs and two dogs. Harry felt so lucky that his aunt and uncle lived on a farm. His stepdad, Mike, was Aunt Judy's brother and the farm was only a twenty-minute walk from Harry's house. He and his mum had moved there two years ago, to be nearer Mike. Harry's mum still talked about the town, and how much she missed the local shops, but Harry loved living in the countryside and getting to spend so much time outdoors.

He put on his coat and followed Aunt Judy past a big ash tree to the feed shed. "I remember how to do it," he said, and began scooping out feed pellets into the bucket.

"It's five scoops each morning, isn't it?" he checked.

"That's right," said Aunt Judy, ruffling his hair. "We'll make a farmer of you yet."

"I think I might want to be one," Harry said seriously. "I love looking after animals."

He lugged the bucket out of the shed towards the chicken coop, glad he was wearing his wellies. It must have rained the night before because the farmyard was full of puddles, and the path to the chicken coop was strewn with mud. Harry's wellies made satisfyingly squelchy noises, and he looked down, enjoying the way the mud oozed out from under them.

"Where's Uncle Martin this morning?" he asked.

"He's still in the milking parlour," said Aunt Judy. "Milking starts at half six, so you've only just missed him. You can go and watch him later, if you like, after you've had your breakfast. It takes a couple of hours to milk the whole herd."

"Great!" said Harry.

"And then in the afternoon, we'd better take Patch and Tilly out for a walk," Aunt Judy went on. "We can walk along the cliff tops."

Harry stopped for a moment to look at the view. His uncle and aunt's farm was near the sea. You couldn't quite see it from the farmyard – just rolling green fields dotted with hedgerows – but on blustery days you could smell the salty tang of it on the wind.

"What are you doing, Harry Lovell?" asked his aunt. "Are you daydreaming?"

"I was trying to smell the sea," said Harry.

"That can be quite tricky over the smell of the cows," laughed his aunt. "Now then, let's feed those chickens."

Harry followed Aunt Judy into the chicken coop and watched as she unlatched the door to let them out of the hen house. They came bustling down the ramp one at a time, their heads bobbing excitedly at the thought of their morning feed. Harry tipped a little bit of grain into each feeding bowl while Aunt Judy freshened up their water. Soon the farmyard was filled with the sound of the peck, peck, peck of beaks against the metal bowls. Strut, the cockerel, swaggered between the hens, occasionally looking at Harry as if to remind him who was boss.

"That Strut is a real character," said Aunt Judy. "He thinks he's king of the farmyard. Now, let's see how many eggs there are."

Harry lifted up the flaps on the hen house, checking each compartment for eggs. "I've got eleven," he cried, as he found the last one, nestled in the straw. It was still warm in his hands and he laid it carefully in his aunt's egg basket.

"How about bacon and eggs for breakfast then?" asked Aunt Judy, smiling.

"Great," said Harry.

He followed his aunt back to the farmhouse, left his boots by the back door, and then went to wash his hands. Patch was looking at him sorrowfully, as if he knew he'd been left out of a treat.

"He's cross because he didn't get to have his morning bark at Strut," said Aunt Judy. "He likes trying to put him in his place," she added, giving Patch a comforting pat.

"Is Strut scared of Patch?" asked Harry.

"No," laughed his aunt. "If Patch barks at Strut then Strut crows right back. Those two would go on for hours if I let them."

"You'd never think it, looking at Patch now," said Harry, stroking his silky smooth head. The dog looked back at him with innocent eyes, as if he'd never barked at anyone in his life.

A tummy full of breakfast later, Harry was back outside again, heading to the milking parlour. Aunt Judy had some morning calls to make and then she was going to clean out the chickens. Even though Harry loved animals, he wasn't too sad to miss that job!

He crossed the yard and went into the huge milking parlour, where Uncle Martin was walking up and down between two rows of big black-and-white cows.

"Hello," he called, waving Harry over. "I've just finished milking this lot," he said, "but I've still got a few more cows to do. They're in the holding yard. Do you want to help?"

"Yes please," said Harry.

His uncle let the first lot of cows back

out into the field beyond the parlour. A moment later, the next lot were coming through the gate, each one lining up in their milking pen.

Harry watched them amble in, admiring their gleaming coats.

"I'll just shut each cow into her pen, then we can get started."

Harry looked at all the tubes beside each pen. Farming was quite a tricky job, he realized.

"Right," said Uncle Martin. "I'll remind you how it goes, shall I? First thing to do is wipe their udders to make sure they're clean. Then we strip off the foremilk and put a cup on each teat."

Harry watched, fascinated, as Uncle Martin attached a tube to each teat. Soon there was a great whirring noise as the milk was sucked down the tube.

"Doesn't it hurt them?" asked Harry.

"Not at all," said Uncle Martin. "They're always eager to be milked. And there's a feeding trough so they can eat at the same time."

Harry spent the next few hours happily trailing after Uncle Martin, watching him at work. After the milking, he helped him clean out the parlour, and then they went to check on the new calves in the field.

"Pizza for lunch," Aunt Judy called, as they finally trooped back into the farmhouse kitchen.

"I could eat ten," said Harry, sinking down at the kitchen table. "Ooh! That smells good," he added, as Aunt Judy pulled the steaming pizzas from the oven. She gave him a huge slice, dripping with melted cheese.

"Yum!" said Harry. "Can I start? I'm starving!"

"It's all the fresh air," said Aunt Judy.

"And all that hard work," added Uncle Martin. "I think we have a young farmer on our hands. You've been a real help this morning, Harry."

Harry beamed with pride.

"Do you still want to come for a walk with me after lunch?" asked Aunt Judy. Then she began to laugh. Harry had taken such a big mouthful of pizza he could only nod.

"Definitely," he said, as soon as he'd swallowed. He heard a faint whining noise and looked down to see Patch, eyeing him hopefully.

"Don't be tricked into giving him any of your pizza," said Uncle Martin.

"He's looking at me like he's never been fed," laughed Harry.

"That's his special act," said Uncle Martin. "He does a very good hungry, orphan dog routine."

Patch gave a very human-like "humph" and slunk back to his basket. He gave Harry one last reproachful glance and curled up next to Tilly.

"I expect you're full after all that pizza," said Aunt Judy, "so you won't be wanting any ice cream for pudding."

"I think I could just manage some," replied Harry, grinning at her. "I'll need extra energy if we're walking Patch and Tilly after lunch."

"I thought you might say that," said Aunt Judy, "so I bought in extra supplies of your favourite – mint chocolate chip."

"Wow! Thanks!" said Harry, but he paused for a moment as he got up to clear the plates. "I just thought – what happens if Mum starts having the baby while we're out?"

"Don't worry, I'll take my mobile with me," said Aunt Judy. "You'll be first to hear the news when it comes in."

After they'd washed the dishes, Harry pulled on his wellies and his thick coat, remembering how windy it could get up on the cliffs. Patch and Tilly barked at him excitedly.

"Off we go!" said Aunt Judy. "And I've got a surprise for you on the way. . ."

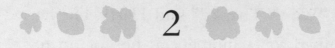

2

Patch and Tilly streaked ahead as soon as they got to the open fields, running in and out of the bushes, scampering over the rocks, noses sniffing the ground, tails wagging in the air.

"They love it out here," said Aunt Judy. "It's definitely their favourite walk."

The next moment, Patch came running up to him, his favourite toy bone in his mouth, and dropped it at Harry's feet. Patch sat down on his haunches and thumped his tail.

"Do you want me to throw it for you?"

asked Harry, looked down at the chewed toy.

Patch barked in reply.

"OK, here goes," said Harry. He picked up the least chewed end of the bone and threw it as far as he could. Patch was after it in a flash, with Tilly yapping at his heels.

"I wonder who'll get there first?" said Harry.

"It'll be Patch," said Aunt Judy. "Tilly's little legs are no match for Patch. She's much older than Patch, too. I always end up bringing two toys so that Tilly's in with a chance. Here's one for Tilly," she added, passing Harry a red ball.

Patch was bounding back towards them, the toy bone firmly in his jaws again. Tilly trotted along behind.

"That was quick!" said Harry. "Right," he said, as Patch dropped the toy at his feet again. "Let's see if I can throw it further this time. And Tilly," he added, showing her the ball, "this one's for you."

This time he had the wind behind him, and Harry watched with satisfaction as the toys sailed through the air. Patch gave a yelp of delight.

As they neared the end of the field Aunt Judy whistled and the dogs came scampering back to her. "Here, Tilly! Here, Patch!" she called, then bent down to put them on their leads.

"Are there sheep ahead?" asked Harry. "Is that why they need to go on their leads?"

"You'll see!" said Aunt Judy, smiling at him. "Could you open the gate for me, Harry?"

Harry did as she asked, then gasped at the amazing view before him. They'd come to the cliff tops, where the ground to their right abruptly dropped away to the pounding sea far below. Harry had never been to this part of the cliff before − his home was further inland − but from here he could see all the way out to sea and hear the waves crashing against the rocks. Herring gulls soared overhead, their squawking cries carrying for miles on the wind. He was glad he'd brought his thick coat, too. It was windy on the cliff tops and Aunt Judy's hair was flying about her face.

"Wow!" said Harry. "What a view. I can see why you don't want Patch and Tilly running near the edge of those cliffs."

"There's a path here we can follow," said Aunt Judy, pointing to a little track a safe distance from the cliff edge. "As long as we stick to the path there's no danger of us falling off the cliffs either!"

"Oh!" said Harry, suddenly remembering. "What was it you were going to show me?"

"You'll have to wait until we've turned the next corner," she said, as they followed the path along the winding cliff edge. "There we are," she cried, a few moments later.

Harry looked to see where Aunt Judy was pointing. There, on the hilly ground to their left, was a whole herd of goats, the white patches on their coats lit up by the sunshine.

"Amazing!" breathed Harry.

As Harry looked more closely, he could see twenty or so goats – some were black and white, others brown and white and there were grey ones and white ones, too, all with different patterns on their coats.

"Oh look!" he cried. "Some of them are huge!" The largest goats had thick horns curving backwards over their heads, and funny little beards under their chins.

"I can't believe there are goats up here. That's awesome!" Harry went on. "But why are they here?"

"They're feral," said Aunt Judy, her face lighting up with pleasure as she looked at them. "I help look after them, actually, along with some other locals."

Aunt Judy saw Harry's puzzled face and explained, "Feral goats live in the wild. They're different from the domestic goats that live on farms. We've got about fifty in this herd."

"That's incredible!" said Harry. "I always thought of goats as farm animals. I didn't know they could live in the wild. But what do they do at night? Where do they sleep?" He looked around at the rocky landscape. *The goats must be really tough to live out here all year*, he thought.

"They sleep under trees, or anywhere they can find shelter. They've got wonderfully thick coats to keep them warm. And of course they can feed themselves on leaves and shrubs. Our main job is to help out with worming and foot trimming from time to time."

"I'd like to do that," said Harry.

"I'll let you know next time we're rounding them up," said Aunt Judy. "It's hard work, but a lot of fun. Sometimes we feed them when the weather's bad, too. They don't like the rain very much, as their coats aren't waterproof. But other than that, they're pretty hardy."

Harry stood watching them for a while. Then he spotted a funny-looking goat standing up on its back legs, trying to reach some leaves on a branch.

"Look at that one!" he cried.

Aunt Judy laughed when she caught sight of the goat. "Sometimes you even see the goats climbing the trees!" she said. "It always takes me by surprise when they do that. It shouldn't though, as they're brilliant climbers. There are goats that live in mountains all over the world – even high up in the Alps and the Pyrenees."

"Mountain-climbing goats!" said Harry. "I'd love to see them one day. Oh!" he added. "What's going on there?"

Two baby goats were leaping up in the air and headbutting each other.

"Those are just baby goats, playing," said Aunt Judy. "The baby goats are called kids.

There's lots of them at this time of year. Those two are boys, practising for when they're older."

Harry looked around, and saw some other kids just ahead of them on the path. They were leaping up a little pile of stones, showing off their climbing skills. Harry loved their inquisitive little faces. "I wish I could go and stroke them," he said.

"I'm afraid they're too wild for that," said Aunt Judy. "I think they'd just run away if you tried to get too close."

As if they'd understood her, the kids looked up at the sound of their voices, then frisked away up the hill, their tails waggling behind them.

Harry looked down at the dogs. They were lying down, tired out after their run up to the cliff tops. "Don't they want to chase the goats?" asked Harry.

"They're more interested in toys and rabbits!" laughed Aunt Judy. "And at this time of year, I think Patch and Tilly are a bit wary of the mother goats. The goats are very protective of their kids. They never let them wander too far. In fact, if you listen, you can probably hear the mothers and kids calling to each other."

"I think I can hear one bleating now," said Harry. "Or is that just the wind?"

"It definitely sounds like a goat," said Aunt Judy, "but that's odd – it seems to be coming from over the cliff."

They stood for a moment, trying to work out the direction the sound was coming from. With the noise of the wind and the waves, it was hard to tell if the bleating came from up ahead or from the way they'd just come.

Aunt Judy stepped forward to investigate, motioning for Harry to keep behind her as they neared the cliff edge. It was just a few feet ahead of them, and Harry could see where the mossy ground crumbled away to nothing.

"Careful, Harry," she said. "There's quite a drop down the cliff. Don't come any further."

"Don't worry, I won't," said Harry, stopping where he was. The bleating cry of the goat came again. "It sounds as if it's scared," said Harry. From where they were standing they could see the rocky face of the cliff below them. There were a few small shrubs clinging to its ledges, but it looked very steep.

"Do you think one of the goats is down there?" he asked.

"I don't know," said Aunt Judy. "The goats rarely go on to the cliffs. The bleating does sound like a distress call though."

Aunt Judy went back to the safety of the cliff path, beckoning for Harry to follow. "Let's go a little further down the path and see if we can catch sight of the goat. We might have a clearer view from there."

Harry scanned the cliff face as they walked. The bleating sound was getting louder and louder, so they must be close now.

"Look, Harry!" cried Aunt Judy. "You're

right, there is one down there. Just beneath that pointy rock."

Harry dropped his gaze and suddenly saw her — a large brown and white goat a little way down from the cliff top. She was standing on a cliff ledge, but it was so narrow, there was hardly any room for her to move. Harry had no idea how she could have got there, let alone how she would get up again.

"She must have got separated from the herd," said Aunt Judy. She turned to the dogs. "Sit, Patch! Sit, Tilly," she said quietly. "We don't want anything to startle the goat," she explained to Harry.

Harry kept his eyes fixed on the goat "She's not trying to climb up the cliff. Oh no!" he said, suddenly realizing what was happening. "I think she's stuck. What are we going to do?"

3

Aunt Judy watched the goat closely for a few more moments. "I just want to see if she can climb up the cliff by herself," she said. But the goat seemed reluctant to move.

"I think we should call the RSPCA," said Aunt Judy. "I could call their 24-hour helpline, but my friend Charlie is the local inspector. He helps me keep an eye on the herd. It might be quicker to ring him. He doesn't live very far away, so he should be able to get to us quickly. Can you take the dogs for a moment?"

She passed Harry the leads and he held on tightly, patting the dogs with his other hand to keep them occupied. It was comforting to stroke Patch's soft coat and to feel Tilly's warm body pressed up against him.

Aunt Judy pulled her mobile phone out of her coat pocket. She flicked through her contacts and clicked on Charlie's number.

Harry waited while the phone rang, willing Aunt Judy's friend to answer. Then came a male voice on the other end of the line.

"Hello, Charlie. It's Judy. Can you hear me?"

She turned her back to the wind as she spoke. "I'm up on the cliff tops," she went on, speaking loudly so she could be heard over the strong gusts of wind. "I'm by the feral goats and it looks as though one of

them is in trouble. She seems to be stuck
on a cliff ledge. Do you think you'd be
able to come and take a look?"

Harry listened while Charlie and Aunt
Judy spoke. She began describing exactly
where they were on the cliffs, which Harry
thought had to be a good sign – Charlie
must have said he'd be able to come.

"That's great," Aunt Judy said at last. "Thanks so much. Yes, we'll wait here."

She put down her phone and gave Harry a reassuring smile. "He's on his way," she said.

"Phew," said Harry. "I'm glad that he's coming. I didn't realize the RSPCA had an emergency service."

"I know," said Aunt Judy. "It's reassuring to know there's someone you can call when an animal's in danger."

"What do we do now?" asked Harry.

"Charlie says we should wait here until he comes, to keep an eye on the goat," Aunt Judy replied.

"I can do that," said Harry.

"We need to keep away from the cliff edge though," said Aunt Judy, "and watch from a safe distance. We don't want the emergency services having to rescue us too!"

Harry and Aunt Judy stepped back a bit so they were safely on the path, but still had the goat in view. Patch and Tilly began tugging at the leads, wanting to see what all the fuss was about.

"Down, Patch. Down, Tilly," said Aunt Judy gently. The dogs sat immediately, but then Tilly began to bark, as if sensing that something exciting was happening.

"I'm going to call Uncle Martin to come and get the dogs," said Aunt Judy. "I don't want them to disturb the goat."

She took out her phone again and didn't have long to wait until Martin answered. "We've found a goat in trouble," she said, keeping her voice calm. "Charlie's going to come and take a look at it, but we're going to stay here until he arrives. Do you think you could come and get the dogs? I'm worried they might startle the goat by barking at her."

Aunt Judy chatted for a while longer,
while Harry gave Patch a quick tummy rub.

"He's going to come straight away,"
said Aunt Judy, slipping her phone back
into her coat pocket. "Do you want me
to take the dogs, or are you OK holding
them?"

"I've got them," said Harry, holding up
his arm so she could see he had the leads
safely wrapped around his hands. Then he
looked back at the goat. She had shifted
her position slightly, but hadn't made it
any further up the cliff face. She had a
distinctive white diamond between her
eyes, and little white patches on her coat.
Otherwise she was a rich, dark brown. He
kept his eyes fixed on the goat, willing
her to look at him, hoping that she might
be comforted by their presence. At last,

she looked up, bleating loudly when she saw them.

"I know, I know," said Harry. "Help is on its way, I promise."

He knew she couldn't understand him, but hoped that at least his voice might reassure her.

"Here comes Martin," said Aunt Judy, pointing to a figure in the distance. Patch and Tilly pricked up their ears at the sound of his name, and started wagging their tails.

Harry was about to wave to him, but Aunt Judy placed her hand on his arm. "We shouldn't make any sudden movements," she said, "or shout. It might scare the goat."

"I didn't think of that," said Harry. He waited for Martin as he came along the path towards them. "I think he's carrying a bag," said Harry, as Uncle Martin approached.

A few moments later and Uncle Martin had reached them. "Hello," he said. "What's the latest? Can you show me where the goat is?"

Harry pointed down to the goat on the cliff face.

"That's odd," said Uncle Martin. "I've never seen a goat get stuck like that. Maybe she's injured. I'm sure Charlie will be able to help though," he added, seeing Harry's anxious expression. "Now, look what I've brought for you two."

He opened his bag to show a couple of scarves, two woolly hats and a pair of binoculars. "I've brought you a thermos of hot chocolate, as well. I thought you might need sustenance on your rescue mission. And it can get quite chilly if you're standing about in these winds."

"Thanks, Uncle Martin," said Harry, handing over the dog leads as Uncle Martin passed him the bag. Harry smiled at him while he sipped on the warming hot chocolate. "But what about the goat?" he said, suddenly. "Won't she be cold and hungry, too?"

"It's OK," said Aunt Judy. "Look — she's got shelter from those overhanging rocks, and there's grass and moss growing in between the cracks in the rocks that she can nibble on."

"Let's take a look through the binoculars," suggested Uncle Martin. "There we are," he said, peering through them. "She's got a little puddle of water to drink so she won't be too thirsty."

"Can I see?" asked Harry.

Uncle Martin handed over the binoculars. "I'd better be getting back to

the farm," he said. "I've got some work
on the hedgerows to do. I'll have a nice
log fire waiting for you when you get
home, though. Come on, Patch. Come
on, Tilly."

He gave Aunt Judy a quick kiss, ruffled
Harry's hair, then set off back to the farm,
the dogs trotting obediently after him.

"Back to our goat duties," said Aunt Judy, pulling on her hat and scarf. "I'm glad Martin brought the hot chocolate," she said, as Harry passed her the thermos. "It's definitely getting chilly out here. Charlie shouldn't be too much longer though."

Harry was busy looking at the goat through the binoculars. "These are amazing," he said. "I can see every detail of her face. Look – she's got orange eyes, and funny-shaped pupils. They look like slits."

He tried focusing the binoculars so he could see the goat even more clearly, but she suddenly disappeared from view.

"Oh!" Aunt Judy cried in surprise.

Harry lowered the binoculars and gasped. The goat had started climbing, picking her way back up the cliff face.

"She's found a way up! I hope she doesn't fall."

"I'm sure she won't," said Aunt Judy. "Goats have suction pads under their hooves that'll help her grip on to the rocks."

Even so, Harry found he was holding his breath as the goat leaped from ledge to ledge. "Please let her make it," he whispered to himself.

Then, with one final bound, she was over the top. Harry stood looking at the goat, standing proudly on the safe ground, and let out a huge sigh of relief. "She made it," he gasped.

4

Harry stayed still for a while. He didn't
want to startle the goat and send her
back down the cliff! The goat didn't seem
to want to move either, though, and was
still bleating loudly.

"I wonder why she still seems
distressed," said Aunt Judy, thinking aloud.
"It didn't seem like she was injured when
she was climbing up the cliff."

"Maybe she's in shock?" suggested Harry.

"Well, at least Charlie can look her
over," said Aunt Judy. "Oh, here he is now,
coming down the path."

Harry looked over to see a tall man dressed in a uniform of navy blue trousers, a black waterproof jacket and stout walking shoes, covered in mud. He had thick, curly black hair and as he came closer Harry could see a badge on his chest, with the letters RSPCA picked out in white.

Aunt Judy walked quickly towards him, and Harry followed.

"Hi, Charlie," she said in a low voice, being careful not to disturb the goat. "I think I may have called you unnecessarily. The goat's just this moment scrambled back up the cliff. She's the brown and white one over there," she added, pointing towards the goat.

"You did right to call me," said Charlie, smiling at Aunt Judy. He had an outdoors sort of face, as if he were used to being out in all weathers. Harry noticed lots of crinkle lines around his eyes as he smiled.

"And this is my nephew, Harry," said Aunt Judy. "He was very helpful at keeping the dogs under control before Martin took them away."

"Hello, Harry," said Charlie. He held out his hand and Harry shook it firmly, suddenly feeling very grown up and responsible. "Thanks for all your help," Charlie continued. "It must have been quite tense keeping watch on her."

"It was," said Harry. "But it was great to know you were on your way. We were worried for a while that she really was stuck down there."

"I'd still like to check her over," Charlie said. He rested his chin in his hand, looking deep in thought for a moment as he gazed at the goat. Harry noticed for the first time that he was wearing a large rucksack. Charlie took it off his back and began having a look through it.

"Are you going to try and catch her?" asked Harry.

"I don't think I'll be able to do that," said Charlie smiling. "I don't know if you've ever seen a goat run, but she'd be far too quick for me. I don't want to distress her either, by giving chase. But," he went on, pulling a small black bucket from his bag, "I'm hoping I'll be able to tempt her over with this."

"What's in it?" asked Harry, peering in.

"Nothing yet," said Charlie. "But I've brought some goat food pellets with me, and with a bit of luck, she'll come to me if I shake them about in the bucket."

The goat already seemed interested in Charlie's bag. Her nose was twitching and she was looking at him inquisitively.

"If we can get her to come over, do you want me to try to keep hold of her while you give her a health check?" asked Aunt Judy.

"I'm hoping she'll stay still for long enough without us having to," said

Charlie, who had already started to pour the goat food into the bucket. He did it as loudly as possible, trying to keep the goat's attention.

"Can I help at all?" asked Harry.

Charlie looked him over, then handed Harry the bucket. "You look like you're up to being part of the team," he said. "I need you to start shaking the food in the bucket, and then walk backwards a little way, very slowly. Hopefully the goat will follow you."

"OK," said Harry. He really hoped their plan was going to work.

"If the goat does come to feed, put the bucket down and step away, keeping your movements small and quiet," said Charlie. "Hopefully she'll be so keen to get to the food, she won't be put off by the rest of us."

Harry felt a little nervous as he started to shake the bucket. He didn't want to trip over or anything, and scare the goat away.

"Come on, girl," he whispered, as he rattled the food around. For a moment, it looked as if the goat wasn't going to be tempted. She stayed exactly where she was, watching Harry closely. But then she began walking slowly towards the bucket, keeping her eyes fixed on Harry all the time.

She picked her way nimbly across the short tufts of grass, until she was in touching distance. Harry couldn't believe he was standing so close to a wild animal. He could hear her breathing and see her sides rising and falling, and the delicate ridges along her curving horns.

At last, her nose was at the rim of the bucket. Holding his breath, Harry put it down on the ground as gently as he could, then stepped away.

Charlie crouched down by the goat's side and began casting an expert eye over her. "She looks to be in good health," he said at last. "Her eyes are clear. Her nose isn't running and her breathing is normal. Her coat looks to be in good condition, too, and so do her hooves."

"But she does seem distressed," Judy pointed out.

Charlie nodded in agreement, and Harry noticed that even though the goat had finished feeding, she wasn't trying to get away from them and join the other feral goats. She kept glancing back towards the cliff face, as if she were looking for something.

"Her udders are full," Charlie commented, still looking her over.

"Does that mean she's got a baby?" asked Judy. "Perhaps that's why she's distressed. She could have been separated from her kid when she went down the cliff."

"She might have one," Charlie replied. "But a goat's udders can fill with milk months after the babies have been suckled, so I can't say for sure."

As he spoke, the goat bleated again and moved back towards the cliff face. "That's odd," remarked Charlie. He looked as if he were deep in thought.

"Perhaps her kid feels too nervous to come back, with us all being here?" suggested Aunt Judy. "Should we go away and try checking on her later today?"

"Our presence shouldn't stop a kid coming to its mother," replied Charlie.

"Is there any other reason the goat could be distressed?" asked Harry. He felt as if this was a puzzle that had to be solved.

"I'm not sure," said Charlie. "We could take her in for a more thorough health check, but that wouldn't be a good idea if she has a kid waiting for her."

Harry suddenly remembered the binoculars Uncle Martin had given him. "I know, I'll use these to look around," he said. "I might be able to spot a kid on its own."

"Good thinking," said Aunt Judy, smiling at him. As Aunt Judy and Charlie talked about what they should do next,

Harry started scanning the horizon. He was able to pick out lots of goats dotted along the horizon, and even some kids on their own, but all of them had adults close by, and none seemed distressed.

Harry swung his binoculars round so they were trained on the goat. She was still standing on the edge of the cliff, and her bleating was growing louder and louder. Harry lowered his vision so he was looking at the cliffs, just like the goat. That was when he saw it – something small and dark on a cliff ledge far below.

"Oh no!" he cried.

"What is it?" asked Aunt Judy, running to his side. A moment later, Charlie was with them, too. "I think. . . Yes, it is. . ." said Harry, as he focused on the spot once more. "There's a baby goat all the way down there. Can you see it?"

Aunt Judy and Charlie looked where Harry was pointing.

"You're right," said Charlie. "That must be her kid." He took a pair of powerful-looking binoculars out of his bag and trained them on the same spot as Harry.

"This is going to be tricky," he admitted. "That kid is clearly stuck, and it's going to need help to make it back on to safe ground."

Harry looked at the small black dot far below the cliff top. Then he looked at the mother goat, calling to her kid. They had to get the kid to safety. But how?

5

Charlie lowered the binoculars and turned back to look at Aunt Judy and Harry. "One thing's for sure, we're not going to be able to do this on our own," he said. "We'll need a specially trained rope team."

"But how will we get one?" asked Harry.

"With a little bit of help from the RSPCA," said Charlie, smiling at him. "They have a rope rescue team made up of specially trained inspectors who have been taught how to rescue animals from tricky situations like this one. They'll be able to abseil down the cliff to reach the kid. I'll give them a call and get a team assembled.

"Will they come straightaway?" asked Harry.

Charlie shook his head. "Not immediately," he said. "It will take some time to get them together, as all the inspectors will need to be excused from their usual duties. I think the best thing would be for you to head home for the night and then we'll regroup in the morning."

"That sounds like a good plan," said Aunt Judy. She could see that Harry was looking worried, so she came over, putting her arm around his shoulders.

"There's no point us waiting here any longer, Harry," she said gently. "We need

to go home, have some supper and get
some sleep. Then we can come back first
thing tomorrow."

Harry looked up at the darkening sky,
and knew Aunt Judy was right. The sun
was hidden behind the clouds now and
it was already getting hard to see the tiny
goat on the cliff. He wouldn't be much
help to it, even if he waited out here
all night. The mother goat didn't look
like she was going to go far though, and

Harry realized that at least if she kept calling, the kid would know its mother was nearby.

He looked over at Charlie. "Do you really think the baby goat will be OK in the night?" he asked. "It's not going to fall or anything, is it?"

Charlie shook his head. "I really don't think that's going to happen, Harry," he said, packing up his rucksack and zipping up his jacket against the wind. "These goats aren't like domestic ones. They're used to being outside in all weathers, and they're made for clambering about on rocks. It'll most likely be sheltering against the cliff wall now."

"OK," said Harry, summoning up a smile.

"Charlie's an expert on goats," added Aunt Judy. "He knows what he's talking about, so there's no need to worry."

"And the overnight wait might even help the rescue," Charlie went on. "The kid will be weaker so it'll be easier to handle. Otherwise it can be tricky trying to get a reluctant goat up a cliff!"

"I can imagine that," said Harry, smiling. He felt a bit happier now. They waved goodbye to Charlie and set off back down the path to home.

The walk home seemed different under the cloudy skies. Turning around for one last peek, Harry couldn't pick out the gleam of the goats' white coats, just their dark shapes, silhouetted against the skyline. They could still hear the sound of the mother goat's bleating being carried on the wind, and Harry guiltily thought of the warm log fire waiting for him back at the farmhouse.

"Hopefully Uncle Martin will have

made our tea by now," said Aunt Judy.
"And he's a much better cook than me."

Harry's tummy rumbled at the mention
of food, and they both laughed. They had
reached the farmyard by now, flooded by
the welcoming lights of the farmhouse
kitchen. They passed the chicken coop,
and Harry could see that the chickens
had already been shut up for the night.
The hens were murmuring to each other
inside as they settled down on their
perches.

"What's the time?" asked Harry,
realizing they'd been out much longer
than he thought.

Aunt Judy looked at her watch.
"It's half six," she replied, "so Uncle
Martin will have finished the afternoon
milking."

She opened the back door and Harry

kicked off his mud-caked wellies, putting them in the cloakroom next to Aunt Judy's. Then he hung up his coat on the peg along with all the others and came through to the kitchen. It was deliciously warm after the windy cliff tops.

Uncle Martin was standing by the cooker and looked up as they came in. "How's the goat?" he asked.

"She managed to climb up by herself," said Harry. "But then we discovered there's a kid down there, too, and it's still stuck on the cliff."

Uncle Martin looked concerned and Aunt Judy quickly filled him in on the rescue plan. Harry was momentarily distracted by the delicious smells from the frying pan. "Yum!" he said, sniffing the air. "I smell sausages!"

"You're right!" said Uncle Martin.
"Sausages, creamy mashed potato and
carrots glazed with honey. Only the best
for the goat rescue team. So," he went on,
"they're going to rescue the baby goat in
the morning?"

"Yes," said Harry. "Charlie said they
need a specially trained rope team to
abseil down the cliff and reach the kid."

"It sounds very dramatic, doesn't it?" said Aunt Judy.

"It does," agreed Harry. "I just wish we could be sure the baby goat is going to be OK."

"How are they going to get the kid back up again?" Uncle Martin wondered.

"I'm not sure," said Aunt Judy. "I hadn't thought of that." Then she caught sight of Harry's anxious glance. "The RSPCA will have done this lots of times before, though. They'll know exactly how to manage. Why don't you feed the dogs, Harry?" she went on. "I think you'll feel much better about the goat if you keep busy."

Patch gave an encouraging bark as Harry stood up, obviously understanding he was about to be fed.

"Come on then," said Harry, calling over to Tilly as well. Aunt Judy was right – he felt much better now he had a job to do.

"Oh, and your mum rang while you were out," Uncle Martin called through to the dogs' room.

"About the baby?" asked Harry excitedly, rushing back in as soon as he'd fed Patch and Tilly.

"It hasn't started coming yet," replied Uncle Martin. "She just wanted to see how you were getting on, so I told her you were out on the cliffs, keeping an eye on a stranded goat."

"Mum will think I'm mad, being this worried about a goat," said Harry grinning. Although his mum liked animals, she was much more interested in things like art and fashion. "Is it OK if I give her a ring?"

"Of course it is," said Aunt Judy. "Give her my love, too."

Harry went through to the sitting room. He was glad it was still quite early, as his mum had started going to bed earlier and earlier. She said the baby kept her awake in the night now, it was kicking so much.

"How's the goat?" she asked, as soon as she answered the phone. "Did you manage to get it to safety?"

Harry filled her in on the latest drama, and how they were leaving the baby goat out on the cliff overnight.

"But there's a specialist rescue team coming tomorrow to get it," Harry finished. "They're going to abseil down the cliff, and Aunt Judy and I are going to watch it happen."

"Oh!" said his mum. "I do hope the baby goat is all right. I'd like to come along and see the rescue, too, but I don't want to risk having this baby on the cliff top!"

"Do you think it's going to come soon, then?" Harry asked eagerly. His mum's due date was today, but before he'd left for the farm, she'd said it could still be a couple of weeks' wait.

"Well, it's always hard to tell, but I hope so! I don't want to be the size of a house for much longer. I'd better go now, love, but I know what you're like, and I don't want you waiting up all night worrying about the baby goat."

"I won't, I promise," said Harry. "I hope the baby lets *you* get some sleep."

"Me, too!" laughed his mum.

Harry went early to bed, wanting to have lots of energy for the goat rescue in the morning. But first he stood for a while, looking out of his bedroom window. It was a beautifully clear night, with no clouds to block the stars. Moonlight flooded on to the farm below. Harry could make out the shapes of the cows in the fields and the rooks roosting in the big ash tree. He thought of the duck by the pond, sitting on her clutch of eggs, and the chickens all cosy in their coop. He thought of his mum, too, safe at home, with her baby still cosily tucked up in her belly. He could only hope it was this still and quiet out on the cliffs. He didn't like to think of the little kid without the warmth of its mother to cuddle up to.

"At least it's not raining," he told himself. "So the kid won't be getting wet." He wondered where the mother goat was, and if she was going to spend all night keeping watch on the cliff top.

"Be safe, little goat," he whispered from his window. Then he climbed into bed, willing the wind and rain to keep away, and for the morning to come quickly.

6

Harry was woken again by Strut the cockerel, his loud crow carrying across the farmyard and right in through his bedroom window. He leaped out of bed, wanting to be in time to meet the RSPCA crew on the cliff top. He didn't want to miss any of the action. And more than anything, he wanted to make sure the baby goat was OK after its night on the cliff face.

He looked around his room, trying to think of all the things he'd need. "Warm clothes," he decided, especially if the rescue was going to take a long time. He put on his thickest trousers, two long-sleeved T-shirts and his big fleecy jumper. Then he pulled his rucksack out from under his bed and put in his woolly hat, scarves, gloves and the binoculars Uncle Martin had lent him yesterday.

As he made his way down the stairs, he could smell toast coming from the kitchen.

"I was just about to check you were up," said Aunt Judy, pouring herself a cup of tea. "Now, what would you like to eat?"

"Toast, please," said Harry, helping himself to a couple of slices. "Have you spoken to Charlie yet?"

"He just rang," said Aunt Judy. "The RSPCA crew are meeting at seven, so you've still got time for breakfast."

Harry was about to sit down when he realized his chair was occupied by a large, one-eyed tabby cat.

"Oh! Sorry!" laughed Aunt Judy. "That's Felix's favourite chair. I'll make him move."

Harry gave Felix a stroke and sat down in the chair next to him. "I don't mind," said Harry. "It's nice to see him again." Felix was famous for keeping his own hours. Sometimes he'd spend days snoozing in the warmth of the kitchen, then he'd disappear for a month, only to return when he was least expected.

"I wonder what he gets up to when he's away," said Harry, helping himself to a spoonful of Aunt Judy's home-made jam.

"I think he has homes all over the countryside," said Aunt Judy. "He always comes back looking very well fed."

As Harry crunched down his toast, Patch and Tilly came racing in from the garden, leaving muddy paw marks all over the kitchen floor. Aunt Judy got up to close the back door, while Harry gave the dogs a morning tummy rub.

"Just what I need – muddy paw prints on the floor. This kitchen is a mess!"

Harry looked around at the higgledy-piggledy kitchen and decided he liked it just the way it was. It looked cosy and lived in.

"Do we need to do anything else before we leave?" asked Harry, clearing away the breakfast things.

"I don't think so," said Aunt Judy. "I've done the chickens already, and your uncle is seeing to everything else."

"Great," said Harry. "I can't wait to get back to the baby goat. I really hope it's been OK in the night." Harry slung on his rucksack, while Aunt Judy packed some biscuits and a thermos of sweet tea in her bag.

"Let's go!" she said. Together they put on their wellies and started out across the farmyard.

Uncle Martin emerged from the

milking parlour as they walked past. "Good luck!" he called. "Let me know how it goes."

"We will," said Harry, waving as they let themselves out of the farm gate. "And will you call if you hear anything from my mum?"

"Of course I will," Uncle Martin reassured him. "Bye now."

It didn't take long to reach the cliff tops, but Harry was amazed by how different the weather felt compared to the farmhouse. It was much windier and colder and he thought again of the baby goat, out in the open all night. White wisps of cloud were scudding across the sky, carried fast by the brisk wind.

The RSPCA team were already assembled at the spot where they'd first seen the mother goat. Harry spotted three men and two women besides Charlie. They all seemed to be very busy. Two of them were handling ropes and harnesses, while another was holding what looked like a stash of metal stakes and a hammer. It all looked very serious.

"Hi!" said Charlie, as they approached the group. "Let me introduce you to everyone. This is Paul and Maya. They're the ones who are going to abseil down the cliff."

Harry smiled shyly at them. Paul, he noticed, was the tallest of them all, his brown hair streaked with grey. Maya had twinkly dark eyes and wasn't that much taller than Harry, but he guessed she must be pretty strong if she was going to abseil down the cliff.

"And this is Helen, Nathan and Ben," Charlie went on. "It's their job to

coordinate the rescue from the cliff top.
They're all experts when it comes to
animal rescue."

Harry smiled again, trying to remember
everyone's names. At first they'd all looked
very similar in their dark, waterproof
clothes and yellow harnesses. Ben, he
noticed, had russet red hair, just like a fox,
and Helen looked like the youngest, her
long blonde hair tied back in a ponytail.

"And," Charlie went on, "everyone, this is Judy and her nephew, Harry. Judy lives at Willowbrook Farm, just east of here. She's been helping out with the goats for a few years now, so she's very familiar with the herd. And Harry is the one who spotted the baby goat on the cliff."

"Good job," said Paul, shaking him by the hand. "If it hadn't been for you and your eagle eyes we wouldn't have known the goat was down there."

"Is the kid OK?" Harry asked him. "Have you spotted it?"

Paul turned around to point to the mother goat who was standing near the cliff path. Harry recognized the small white diamond between her eyes and her lovely rich brown coat, flecked with white.

"We're hoping she's going to guide us to it," said Paul. "We can't see the kid, but the mother goat keeps calling to it, so we're sure her baby must be down there somewhere."

As he spoke, Harry noticed that Maya had her binoculars trained on the cliff, following the gaze of the mother goat. "I can see it!" she said suddenly.

"Where?" asked Charlie. Harry and Aunt Judy moved closer to Maya, who was pointing down the cliff face.

"Yes, there it is," said Maya. "You can just see it without the binoculars. It looks as though the kid is hiding in a little hole on the ledge."

"I can see it now!" said Harry, relief flooding through him that the baby goat was still there. He quickly pulled his binoculars out of his rucksack and trained them on the kid. Only its head was visible, peering out of the hole on the ledge.

"It's so far down," said Aunt Judy. "If it weren't for the mother goat, we'd have had a lot of trouble spotting it."

"What happens now?" asked Harry. "Is the kid going to be hard to reach?"

"It's not going to be easy," admitted Charlie. "We still need to work out the best strategy. So far, we know we're going to need two abseilers, one on either side of the kid, in case it moves. We're then going to try and get it back up in this bag."

Charlie held up the bag for Harry to see. It was made out of a dark green canvas and it looked very sturdy. "We're going to attach the bag to an abseiler's harness on the way down, then on the way back up we'll attach it to a pulley system, which Nathan is putting in at the top of the cliffs."

"It's the coming back up that's the hardest part," Maya added. "You're less in control as you're being pulled up. And we'll have to be extra careful if we've got a baby goat in tow." As she spoke she put a hard hat over her short brown hair, then she and Paul tightened their harnesses and made sure all the rope knots were secure. The rest of the RSPCA crew stood in a huddle, talking and pointing, and clearly trying to work out the best route down the rocks to the kid.

Harry and Aunt Judy could only watch and wait while the team talked everything over, but it wasn't long before Charlie came over to explain their action plan.

"Right," he said, rubbing his hands together. "We're going to use a rope anchor system. That means Paul and Maya will each be attached by two ropes to those metal stakes at the top of the crag." Harry looked over to see Nathan pounding in some metal stakes at the top of the cliff with a sturdy-looking hammer. "The first rope is the abseil rope, so they'll use that to get down."

"What about the second rope?" asked Aunt Judy.

"That's the safety rope. Paul and Maya will have one attached to either end of their harnesses as a backup. Ben and Nathan will keep a hold of the abseil rope, and they'll be in charge of letting the rope out or pulling it in, to help Paul and Maya on their way. Helen's going to guide them down."

Harry looked over at Paul and Maya, who were preparing for the descent. It looked terrifying, even if they were attached by lots of ropes.

"It all sounds quite complicated," said Harry.

"Don't worry," said Charlie, confidently. "Everyone here has had lots of training, so they all know what they're doing. I will have to ask you to both stay back here while we do the rescue operation. That way, I won't have to worry about your safety, and we'll keep this zone clear to concentrate on the rescue."

"Of course," said Aunt Judy. "We only want to help, not get in the way."

Harry couldn't help feeling a little disappointed that he wasn't going to be able to see the rescue as it happened, but he knew it was important they left the inspectors to get on with their job.

"Don't worry," said Charlie. "I'll keep you informed as we go."

At that moment, Helen gave a wave. "They're going down!" she called.

Harry watched, his heart in his mouth, as Paul and Maya leaned backwards over the cliff, their faces tilted up at the sky, and then disappeared from view.

7

Harry looked down and realized he was holding Aunt Judy's hand so tight that his knuckles had turned white. "Sorry!" he said.

"That's OK," said Aunt Judy. "I think I've been gripping your hand, too. It's quite something seeing two people disappear over a cliff like that."

They could still hear Paul and Maya calling up to the others. Maya was asking for more rope, and as the wind died down, Harry could make out the noise of their thick climbing boots banging against the cliff face.

"If you stand over there, you'll be able to see them going down the cliff for a little while longer," said Charlie, pointing to his left.

As Harry and Aunt Judy walked further down the cliff path for a better look, Harry caught sight of the mother goat again. Harry realized guiltily that he'd forgotten all about her in the excitement of the rescue mission. She seemed to know something was about to happen, and was calling more and more urgently to her kid. He wished he could go up and stroke her, as he would if it were Patch or Tilly, but he knew that as a wild animal, it wouldn't soothe her at all.

"She's a brilliant mum, isn't she?" said Aunt Judy, watching her as they walked past. "She must be exhausted, too, if she's been out here all night."

Harry couldn't help imagining how worried his mum would be if he were the one stuck on the cliff face.

"It's amazing how strong the mother instinct is," agreed Charlie. "Poor thing – I should imagine she's pretty stressed right now. The sooner we get the kid back to her the better."

"How's it going?" Aunt Judy called over to the others.

"Not long to go now," answered Helen, who was still busy guiding Paul and Maya towards the goat. "They're going down steadily."

From his new position, Harry could just see the gleaming yellow tops of Paul and Maya's climbing hats, bobbing down the cliff face. They already seemed very far away.

The cliff face wasn't flat, Harry realized,

now that he was looking at it properly, but strewn with ridges and lumpy boulders that stuck out at crazy angles.

"Is it quite difficult to get down — because of the way the rocks stick out?" asked Harry.

"It is," said Charlie. "Abseiling is actually much easier on a flat surface, as then you can just sit back and bounce your way down. But Paul and Maya will really need to concentrate going down over this lot, and work out where to put their feet so they get the right balance."

"I'm glad it's not me going down there," Aunt Judy admitted.

"It's much safer than it looks," said Charlie. "They're attached by two ropes, remember, and there's a braking system in case anyone accidentally lets go."

Aunt Judy didn't look convinced, but Harry found himself thinking that he'd love to learn to abseil. It would be amazing to be good enough to go on rescue missions. Although whenever he leaned forward for a better look, it did make his head swim a bit. The cliffs dropped away to nothing but air, with only the pounding waves far, far below.

"How is Maya going to be able to get

the baby goat in the bag?" Harry asked, suddenly. "She'll need to keep one hand holding on to the rope, won't she?"

"No, that would make the rescue much harder! She'll need both hands to catch the kid. To do that, we just put the brakes on so she can stay in the same position without having to hold on with her hands."

Charlie paused for a moment to see how far away Paul and Maya were from the baby goat.

"They're making really good progress," he reported back. "Now, where was I? Oh yes – the bag. It's attached to Maya's harness, so she can grip the goat in her hands and put it into the bag. And she'll make sure Paul is waiting at the other end of the ledge, so if the kid tries to run, he can make a grab for it."

"Do you think the kid will try to

run away?" asked Harry. "That could be dangerous, couldn't it?"

"It could," admitted Charlie, "but I shouldn't think it will. The kid's been out on the cliff all night, so won't have fed for a while. I'm hoping it'll be feeling too weak to try to run away. It's good that it's hiding in that hole, too, as that should make it easier for Maya to catch it."

Charlie moved forward to chat to Ben and Nathan, who were still holding their position at the cliff edge.

"It seems to be taking a long time, doesn't it?" Harry said to Aunt Judy.

"I know," Aunt Judy replied, "but that's only because we're so anxious. It's making a few minutes seem like years. But I'm sure everything is going according to plan."

As she spoke she passed Harry the thermos of sweet tea. "Here, have this," she said. "It will make you feel better — and warm you up!"

"Thanks!" said Harry, absent-mindedly taking it from her. He didn't want to take his eyes off the baby goat for a moment. He somehow thought that if he kept focusing on the rescue he'd be able to help in some way.

He felt much better, though, as he took a gulp of tea and the warm liquid slipped down his throat. But then he looked over at the inspectors and froze. They were all waiting on the cliff ledge in tense silence, their concentration fixed on a point far below them.

"Oh, no!" said Harry. "Has something gone wrong?"

Charlie glanced back at them, a pair of binoculars in his hands. "They're level with the kid now," he said, dropping his voice to a whisper. "Maya's trying to get along the ledge to reach it. It's very important she doesn't startle it."

He turned his attention back to the rescue. Harry wanted to move forward to see what was happening, but Aunt Judy stopped him. "Not too close to the edge, Harry," she reminded him.

"You're right, sorry," said Harry. "I just wish I could see what was happening."

This last wait was the most anxious of all. Harry wondered why it was taking so long for Maya to reach the kid. His worst fear was that the kid would jump when it saw Paul and Maya coming.

"Brilliant!" cried Charlie, who was now glued to his binoculars.

Aunt Judy grinned at Harry. "That sounds good," she said.

"Maya's got the kid," Charlie went on,

still looking through his binoculars. "She's got a good grip on it — one hand under the neck, the other gripping the back legs — that's perfect. And she's putting it in the bag. Hooray — it's in. Fantastic!"

"Are they coming back up?" asked Harry.

"Yes!" said Charlie. He turned to them, smiling, giving the thumbs up. "She must think the kid is light enough to keep the bag attached to her harness, so I don't think we're going to need to winch it up. Now it's time for them to start the ascent."

8

Harry waited tensely for the RSPCA inspectors to emerge at the top of the cliff. He knew this was the trickiest part – coming back up over the jutting boulders and crumbling rocks. *What happens if the tiny goat falls out of the bag?* he thought. *Or if Maya slips and the kid is banged against the rocks?*

He knew he should stop worrying. The RSPCA were trained for this, after all. But it was just so difficult when there was nothing he could do to help.

Ben and Nathan were hard at work,

pulling the ropes back up, while Helen pointed out the easiest route for Paul and Maya to take.

The mother goat had come forward, and was standing at the very edge of the cliff now, bleating repeatedly, her tail swinging from side to side.

At last, Harry caught sight of the white helmets again, then Maya came into view. "Look!" Harry cried. "I can see the kid!" Its little black head was peering out of the green bag, a bewildered expression on its face. Harry couldn't believe how tiny it was. It looked so vulnerable.

The mother goat's bleating took on a different tone now. She sounded much less distressed and more excited. She began impatiently pacing along the cliff. Harry wished he could hold her back, as she seemed dangerously near the edge.

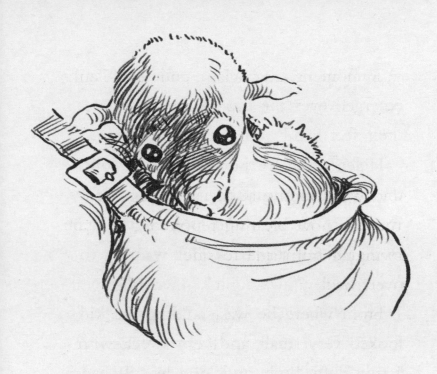

He crossed his fingers, desperately
hoping the baby goat would be all right.
Then he heard it – a very faint bleating –
as the baby goat called back to its mother.

"That's a good sign, isn't it?" asked
Harry, glancing over at Aunt Judy.

She smiled back at him. "It definitely
is," she replied. "It can't be that weak if
it's still trying to call to its mother."

A moment later, Maya, and then Paul, emerged over the top of the cliff face, their feet firmly on flat ground again.

Helen came forward and helped open the bag, lifting out the baby goat. Harry wanted to rush up and look at it, but he made himself stay back, not wanting to overcrowd it.

From where he was standing the kid looked very small, and very sweet, with a tiny fluffy body and long legs. It had a black face and grey and white markings on its body, and it kept giving little high-pitched bleats as Helen held it in her arms. The mother goat kept a wary distance from the inspectors, but her eyes were fixed on the kid.

Then the team fell silent, all of them watching Helen as she handled the baby goat.

"Is it OK?" Harry asked.

"Well, I can confirm it's a boy," said Helen. "And I think he's only around three to five days old, so I'd say he's had a very lucky escape. I'm not sure how long he could have survived out there on his own. It's a good thing you and Judy spotted him when you did. And that you got in touch with us so quickly."

She continued to run her hands gently over the kid's body, then his legs, testing for any sign of breakages.

"What do you think, Helen?" asked Charlie.

"He looks to be in good condition," Helen replied. "Good skin, nice clear eyes. He seems very light and weak, but then he would after so long without food. I can't see anything wrong with him, so I think the best thing is to get him back to his mother."

As she spoke, she stood up, holding the kid close to her body, and walked over to Aunt Judy. "Would you like to give him back to his mother?" she asked. "After all, you're the most familiar with the herd."

"Oh, thank you," said Judy, beaming at her.

She held out her arms and very carefully took the baby goat from Helen. "Oh, isn't he gorgeous?" she whispered. Harry stood by her side, and gave the kid a tiny stroke. He had a lovely sooty-black face, with amazing orangey-yellow eyes, a little pink nose and sweet little sticky-out ears. Harry was amazed by how soft his hair felt. His hooves looked very big compared to the rest of his body, as if he was going to have to grow into them.

"I can't think how he even got down there in the first place," said Judy, "if he's so young."

"Baby goats can walk very soon after birth," said Helen. "And they're born climbers. I should think this is the mother's first kid, though. Her inexperience meant that she didn't realize the slope would be too tricky for her kid to manage."

"Well, she will have learned her lesson," Nathan pointed out. "She was up all night worrying about him, so I'd say she's got the makings of a very good mother."

"Why did she go down there?" asked Harry.

"She was probably after some juicy plants," laughed Charlie. "Goats will do anything for food. Even scale near-perpendicular cliff faces!"

The tiny goat gave a little bleat, as if in agreement, and they all looked over at him. "He's so sweet, isn't he?" said Harry, thinking how amazing it was that the goat had managed to get down the cliff at all, when he had only just been born.

"He is," said Aunt Judy, "and sadly it's time for me to give this tiny little thing back to its mother, however tempting it is to keep cuddling him."

Aunt Judy walked over to the mother goat and gently set the kid down by her side, then stepped back.

Everyone held their breath for a moment, willing the mother goat to accept him. Harry knew that if baby animals were away from their mothers for too long, they risked being rejected by them. But the baby goat gave a little bleat and immediately started nudging at its mother's teats, before suckling thirstily on her milk. The mother goat turned her head to nuzzle her kid, then stayed perfectly still.

Harry looked over at Aunt Judy and saw that she had tears in her eyes. She caught his glance and they smiled at each other.

"We should name him," Harry said. "He deserves a name after all his adventures."

"How about Cliff?" suggested Paul.

Helen gave him a nudge with her elbow. "That's a terrible joke," she said.

"What about Sooty?" suggested Judy, looking at the black markings on his face.

"That's a perfect name," said Charlie, watching the mother and kid together.

Harry thought he'd remember this moment for a long time. Just then Sooty came away from his mother and looked at them all, twitching his little pink nose. Then, as if he had satisfied his interest, he turned back to the important task of getting more milk from his mother.

"Well, we'd better be packing up,"
said Ben, and the RSPCA team began
collecting their equipment, pulling out the
metal stakes and carefully winding up the
ropes before putting them in their huge
backpacks.

"We'll check these thoroughly when
we get back to base," Charlie explained,
"to make sure the ropes haven't been
damaged."

Harry turned back to look at Sooty
who was still busy feeding, his little tail
wagging happily.

"I wish I had a camera," said Harry. "Then I could take a photo of Sooty to show to Mum."

"I know," said Aunt Judy. "We can use my phone." She pulled her mobile out of her pocket and took a photograph. "Look at this," she said.

Harry peeked over her shoulder. "Brilliant!" he grinned. "Although you can't see much of Sooty's face. We'll have to try to take another one when he's finished feeding."

"I don't think that's going to be any time soon," laughed Aunt Judy. "Poor little thing must be starving."

"Are we just going to leave them now?" asked Harry.

"Well, I'll definitely come back and check on them over the next few days," replied Aunt Judy. "Just to make sure

they're getting on OK. I don't think there
are going to be any problems though."

Harry and Aunt Judy began walking
back with the RSPCA team towards their
Land Rover, which was parked nearby on
the coastal path. "I think Sooty and his
mum are going to be just fine," Charlie
agreed as they loaded up. "But if there are
any problems, you know you can always
ring me."

"Thanks," said Aunt Judy, smiling at
him. "That's good to know. Would you all
like to come back to Willowbrook Farm?
I made a cake this morning, just in case
we had something to celebrate."

"That would be lovely," said Paul. "I
think we could all do with a cup of tea."

"We've got a bit of space in the Land
Rover," Charlie added. "Harry, would you
like to ride back with us?"

"Really?" said Harry, a grin spreading over his face. "That would be brilliant. If that's OK, Aunt Judy?"

"Of course it is," said his aunt. "I'll see you all back at the farm."

As Aunt Judy walked back down the cliff path, Harry climbed into the back of the Land Rover. Charlie took the driving seat, next to Helen, and the rest of the RSPCA team sat squashed in together in the back. As they drove off, Harry glanced anxiously out of the window, eager for one last look at Sooty and his mum.

Just before they turned the corner, he caught a glimpse of the tiny goat. He had finished feeding and was trotting happily along behind his mother, away from the cliff. The mother goat's brown coat was quickly lost among the shrubs and boulders, but Harry could still see Sooty,

the white patches on his coat gleaming
against the grey rocks. The kid gave
a little skip, then followed his mother
into the long grasses, until he finally
disappeared from view.

Harry kept watching, to see if they
would reappear, but they were lost in the
landscape. "Goodbye, Sooty!" he called. He
knew the goats wouldn't understand him,
but it felt wrong to leave without saying

goodbye. He turned to see that Paul had been watching along with him. "I feel sort of sad that they've gone," admitted Harry.

"I know," Paul replied. "But you'll be able to visit them again. "And it's going to be a great story to tell!"

"That's true!" said Harry. "I can't wait to tell my mum about it. I'm only sorry it wasn't me who abseiled down the cliff to rescue the kid. I think I've changed my mind about wanting to be a farmer. I want to be an RSPCA inspector, so I can do animal rescues. That would be so cool."

Paul laughed. "I think you'd be brilliant," he said.

"How did you become an inspector?" Harry asked.

"Well," said Paul. "I started out volunteering at one of the RSPCA centres, and then I got so hooked I applied when a job came up to be an RSPCA worker. And I loved it – looking after the animals at the centre, helping to rehabilitate the ones that could be released back into the wild. Then I got interested in how animals are protected by law and I wanted to help people learn how to care for their animals, so after that I applied for a place on an inspector training course."

"Wow," said Harry. "It sounds like you've had a lot of experience. Is it very hard work?"

"It is," agreed Paul. "But it's exciting, too. You never know how your day is going to turn out when you're an inspector. Sometimes I'm dealing with complaints about people not caring for their animals properly, or educating people about animal welfare. And sometimes it's dramatic animal rescues — cats up trees, stranded dogs. . . We even had to rescue a squirrel trapped in a drainpipe once! I don't know how it managed to get so far up. But the best times are ones like we had today. It's the kind of moment you always hope for, and no matter how many animal rescues we've done, it's always incredibly rewarding when it happens."

"I'd love to do that kind of work," said Harry.

"Well, I can see you already care a lot about animals," said Paul. "Helping out on your uncle's farm is giving you lots of experience. And when you're old enough, you could do volunteer work, too."

"That would be great," said Harry.

"Are you peppering Paul with questions?" laughed Charlie, as he navigated the Land Rover down the twisting lane towards the farm.

Harry nodded, with a grin. "I'm finding out all about how to become an RSPCA inspector," he said. "But perhaps I should give Paul a break!"

"You mean you've got more questions?" asked Paul, with a look of mock horror.

"Loads more," said Harry.

"What else did you want to know?" asked Charlie.

"I want to know more about the rope rescue team," said Harry. "Did you have to do special training for it?"

"Oh yes," said Helen, turning round to look at Harry. "Don't remind me," she said, doing a mock eye roll. "I had four very wet days of it. And my instructor was really strict."

"Hey," interrupted Charlie. "I was your instructor."

"I know," laughed Helen. "I'm teasing. Actually, you were the best." She looked back at Harry. "It was great – we learned all about rope rescue techniques, and about the different types of rope, how to tie knots and the safety and checking procedures. There was a test at the end of it all, to make sure we could set up a rope system and use it to rescue an animal."

"Did you get to rescue a real live animal, then?" asked Harry.

"No," said Charlie. "That would have been too risky. We used soft toys instead!"

"I seem to remember I had to rescue a cuddly crocodile from a cliff ledge. Not something I'm likely to have to do again."

By now, they were drawing up at the farmhouse. Harry leaped down and they all trudged inside, taking off their coats and boots in the cloakroom and coming through to the welcoming warmth of the kitchen. Aunt Judy was already there, getting down the big teapot from the dresser.

"You beat us!" said Harry.

"I know," crowed Aunt Judy. "You've been driving down all those winding country lanes. I only had to walk back across the field. Make yourselves at home everyone," she went on, gesturing towards the kitchen table. "You'll have to get past the dogs first though," she laughed.

Patch and Tilly rushed around saying hello to everyone, wagging their tails and enjoying all the attention.

"I'll just go and get that cake," said Aunt Judy, placing the tea on the table.

Harry followed her through to the larder. "Do you think Sooty will remember it all?" he asked. "Do you think he'll remember us?"

"I don't know," said Aunt Judy. "I'm not sure how long goats remember things for. I wouldn't be surprised if he's a bit wary of cliffs from now on."

"Can we go back to the cliffs though, after the baby's been born? I'd love to see Sooty again."

"Of course," said Aunt Judy. "And then you can show him off to your new baby brother or sister."

Harry went to the cupboard and took

down the chipped enamel mugs and an assortment of brightly coloured plates. He brought them to the table on a tray, along with the milk, while Aunt Judy set the teapot down on the table. Then the kitchen door banged open again.

"Perfect timing," said Aunt Judy, as Uncle Martin came in. "Come and join us for cake."

"So what happened?" asked Uncle Martin, settling himself down on one of the comfy chairs around the table.

"A successful goat rescue," said Charlie, shaking him by the hand. "The kid is back with his mother, happy and healthy."

"We've named him, too," put in Harry. "He's called Sooty."

"Fantastic news," said Uncle Martin. "You'll have to point him out to me next time we're on the cliffs."

"Sorry for all this mess," Aunt Judy apologized, as she began trying to hand out slices of cake amidst all the clutter. "What with all the farm work and the goat rescues, there never seems to be any time for tidying up."

"Well, I think you've got your priorities right," laughed Charlie.

"And you found time to make a cake," added Maya. "I think that's pretty impressive."

"This milk is about as fresh as it gets," added Uncle Martin. "That's what you get when you come to a dairy farm for tea."

"And this cake is delicious," said Paul, tucking into a huge slice. "Thank you!"

"I think we should have a toast," said Charlie, once the tea had been poured. "To the goat rescuers!"

"To the goat rescuers!" everyone cried, clinking mugs.

At that moment, the telephone rang in the background, but Harry hardly noticed it, he was so busy hearing all about how Helen had continued training with a local inspector. Then he heard Aunt Judy's soft voice in his ear.

"Phone for you, Harry," she said.

"Oh!" said Harry, jumping up and taking the receiver.

"Hello?" he said.

"Harry, guess what!" cried his mum. "You're a big brother at last! The baby's come!"

"Hooray!" cried Harry, punching the air.

"And it's a boy," his mum went on.

"Yes!" Harry cried again.

His mum laughed.

"Have you chosen a name yet?" asked Harry.

"Leo," replied his mum. "What do you think? Do you like it?"

"I do. I can't wait to meet him."

"Aunt Judy says she's going to drive you over, later tonight."

Harry chatted to his mum for a little while longer, then she passed the phone to his stepdad, who sounded over the moon. Finally, Harry rang off, smiling as he put down the phone.

"I've become a big brother!" he announced to everyone.

"Congratulations!" cried Uncle Martin, and everyone made another toast with their mugs of tea.

"This has been the best day ever," Harry declared. "We've rescued a baby goat and I've got a new baby brother. It can't get better than that."

Epilogue

A month later, Harry was walking along the cliff tops to Willowbrook Farm. Only this time, he had his mum, stepdad and baby brother Leo with him. Leo was wrapped up against the cold in a fleecy blanket, a little tuft of dark hair peeping out from under his woolly hat.

Harry was extra excited – not only could he show everyone where they'd rescued the goat, but Aunt Judy had rung to say that the duck's eggs had hatched, and they now had six fluffy ducklings swimming about on the farm pond.

His stepdad was carrying Leo in a sling, and Harry kept going over to take a peek at him, trying to make him smile by tapping him very gently on the nose.

"I nearly got one!" he said.

His stepdad laughed. "He's still very young for a first smile," he said. "Be patient. I'm sure it'll come soon."

"I know," said Harry. "I just want to be there to see it when it happens."

"Well, we already know how much he likes you," said his stepdad. "You can tell by the way he kicks his legs whenever you come into the room."

"Perhaps when we're older, we can train to be RSPCA inspectors together," Harry declared.

Harry's mum groaned. "Two animal-mad boys! That's all I need! Who's going to come shopping with me?"

"Sorry, Mum," laughed Harry. "Not me."

"I'm not giving up yet," said his mum. "Now, where is the spot of the famous goat rescue? I've heard so much about it, I'd love to see where it all happened."

"Just over there!" said Harry, pointing to the cliff ledge where they'd first seen the mother goat standing. "And the baby goat, Sooty, was all the way down there." He pointed to the cliff ledge far, far below.

"Wow," said his mum. "That's amazing that the RSPCA managed to abseil all the way down there. And even more impressive that they were able to get back up again with the kid."

"And there are the goats," added his stepdad, pointing to the herd as they came into view, ambling along the cliff top paths.

"Can you see Sooty?" asked his mum. Harry had described the goats to her in detail. "The mother is brown and white, isn't she? And Sooty's grey and white with black legs and black markings on his face."

"That's right!" said Harry. "I don't know if I can see them though," he added, his eyes flicking through the herd, longing for a glimpse of them.

The goats came to a stop a little distance away from them, and began grazing on the leafy shrubs.

"There they are!" cried Harry suddenly, his eyes lit up with joy. There was the mother – he was sure it was her, recognizing her rich brown coat and the white diamond between her eyes. By her side was a little kid, though not nearly so tiny as a month ago.

"Look how much Sooty's grown," said Harry. He looked strong and healthy, frisking about on his gangly legs.

As they passed by, the mother goat looked up as if in recognition.

"She knows me!" cried Harry. "I'm sure of it!"

He gazed at both the goats for a moment, then came over to Leo. "Can I take him out of his sling, to show him the goats?" he asked.

"Of course you can," said his stepdad, passing Leo over to him.

"Leo, meet Sooty and his mum," he said, turning Leo around so he could see the goats. "I'll tell you all about them when you're older."

As he spoke, Sooty gave a little bleat and Leo smiled.

"Did you see that?" cried Harry, delighted. "Leo's first smile."

Harry's mum laughed. "Amazing!" she said. "That confirms it – I'm definitely going to have two animal-mad boys."

Then the goats turned and began to run back through the tussocky grass. Harry watched them go – happy at the sight of the mother goat and her kid, gambolling under the spring sky. Soon they were lost among the rest of the herd, and Harry smiled as their bleating mingled with the screeching of the seagulls and the distant sound of the waves, crashing against the rocks far below. Harry knew these cliffs would always be a special place for him – a reminder of the day he was lucky enough to see the rescue of a tiny goat and welcome his little brother into the world.

The Real-Life Rescue

Although the characters and animals in Harry's story are fictional, they are based on a real-life rescue in which a baby goat was stranded on a cliff face.

An RSPCA rescue team had to abseil thirty metres down Castle Rock in Lynton, Devon, to rescue a baby goat stranded and separated from its mother. When the team arrived, the mother goat had already made it back to the top on her own, but her newborn kid was not with her. Two RSPCA inspectors, Marija Zwager and Will Hendry, abseiled down to the ledge and, after searching for some time, they found the frightened youngster hiding in a tiny hole on a ledge. The kid was put into a bag carried by RSPCA Inspector Hendry, and with assistance from RSPCA Inspector Zwager, they climbed back to the top. Once back on firm ground, and a safe distance from the cliff edge, the kid was reunited with its mum and within moments was happily feeding, no worse for the ordeal.

The very steep cliff face

Photo by Andrew Forsyth/RSPCA Photolibrary

RSPCA inspectors plan the rescue

The mother goat

Back on safe ground! Inspector Zwager
holding the tiny goat

Photo by Andrew Forsyth/RSPCA Photolibrary

Meet A Real RSPCA Inspector
- Marija Zwager

You were part of the real-life rescue that Harry's story is based on. Can you tell us a bit more about the rescue?
The goat colony is feral, and looked after by a group of locals. The RSPCA help regularly with monitoring them and helping worm them. The locals called the RSPCA out to help them after they had monitored the nanny [female goat] and realized she had kidded [had a baby]. She gave birth on a tricky ledge, and while she was able to climb back up, the kid wasn't strong enough to. The mother goat was then seen calling to the kid and becoming quite distressed. She also had exceptionally full udders and if the RSPCA hadn't intervened she could have had health problems, too.

By watching the mother calling to the kid, we were able to establish roughly where the kid was. Me and another officer then abseiled down, one from each side in case the animal moved. Once we reached the kid, we were able to put it in a bag and hoist it up with us.

What was the trickiest part of the rescue?
The trickiest part of the rescue was finding where the kid was on the cliff face and making sure we didn't startle the kid as we approached. As we were coming down the cliff edge we had to move very slowly and carefully. The ledge was so small we didn't want the kid to back away and fall off accidentally. It was also hard to communicate with the rest of the team because we didn't have very good radio signal and the wind was quite strong.

Why did you want to work for the RSPCA?
When I joined the RSPCA ten years ago I

wanted to do a job that meant something, and that is still true today. I always loved animals, and working for the RSPCA means that I get to do something I believe in every day.

How do you train to become a RSPCA inspector?

All our new inspectors are trained in rope rescue techniques during their basic training. This is four full days in North Wales where the trainee inspector will learn about the different types of rope and their uses, tying knots and where and when the knots should be used, as well as lots of safety and checking procedures. At the end of the four days, the new inspectors are required to pass a practical test where they each demonstrate that they can set up a rope system and use it effectively to rescue (usually soft toys dropped on to ledges).

Those inspectors who have passed and join

their regional rescue teams, will train with their local inspectorate rescue team on a regular basis. Currently we have three rope-rescue teams around England and Wales.

Could you describe a typical day at work?

As I am part of the specialist rope team, my days are usually planned in advance – i.e., the animal may have been stuck for over a day, so the call goes out to the inspectors with specialist rope skills and the team is assembled and the abseil/climb planned. This small delay can help, as the animal is more tired by the time we get there so less likely to resist rescue attempts! So it's a bit different from some of the other teams who have to react quickly.

Four or five members of the team assemble, gathering together ropes, harnesses, helmets, walkie talkies, radios, bags to put the animal in, and stakes, etc. We drive as close as possible to the rescue, then walk with the equipment the rest of the way.

What is the best thing about being an RSPCA inspector?
The best thing about my job is when an animal is OK after rescuing them from a really tricky climb. It was a really heart-warming moment on this particular rescue when the mum goat started calling out to the kid as soon as she saw it and the kid immediately started to suckle when it was put next to the mum. It was just brilliant.

To find out more about the work
the RSPCA do, go to:
www.rspca.org.uk

Facts About Goats

- Baby goats are called "kids".

- Female goats are called "does" or "nannies" and male goats are called "bucks" or "billies".

  A group of goats is called a "trip".

- Goats can be born with or without horns.

- Both male and female goats often have beards, and dangly flaps of skin on their neck known as "toggles", "wattles" or "tassels".

  Goats are very good at climbing. They can climb very steep cliff faces and can even climb trees!

Goats are able to rear up on their back legs to reach food growing above them.

Goats don't like to get wet and prefer to seek shelter during bad weather.

Pygmy goats are naturally tiny goats. They usually grow to around 40-56 cm.

Goat's milk is used for drinking, cooking and baking. It is whiter than whole cow's milk.

Based on a real-life animal rescue

RSPCA

The Lonely Pony

Buying this book helps the RSPCA save animals' lives

Take a sneak peek at another
exciting story based on a
real–life animal rescue!

As they arrived at the centre, Mia breathed in the smell of hay and horses and gave a huge grin. Today was the day she was going to meet Polly! Mum opened the gate, and they walked inside. Mia looked round at the familiar surroundings. There were four stable blocks around a big yard and a long wooden shed where Mum and the rest of the RSPCA grooms had their offices. Next to that was a picnic area with a little hut that they used as a shop, selling horse posters, second-hand books and ice creams to the visitors.

It was already open for the day, and Mia could see two ladies inside having a cup of tea and a chat. Two of the RSPCA grooms, Helen and Lynn, were sweeping the yard, and Ali was feeding the donkeys. Past the stables were the paddocks, and in each one, there were three or four horses, chomping the grass happily. Over in one of the training fields, Mia could see Amanda cantering Beans.

Mia grinned as she saw the little bay horse. Beans had only just arrived and still needed lots of work. He was terrified of loud noises, and couldn't go anywhere near traffic without getting really scared. But he loved his groom, Amanda, and he was getting better every day.

"I've got to call the vet, then I'm going straight up to check on Polly."

Mum nodded her head over to the isolation stables. "Give me ten minutes or so to make sure she's all right, then come and join us. Polly's in the last stable."

"OK!" Mia grinned. That gave her just enough time to say hello to all her friends! She went over to the nearest paddock and drummed her hands on the wooden fence. The three young mares, Honey, Star and Dapple, all looked up at the noise. "Hello, girls!" Mia called.

The largest mare started cantering over.

"Hi, Honey!" Mia called. The gorgeous golden palomino horse had come over to the side of the paddock to see her. Mia reached up to stroke her on the neck. Honey huffed happily, and swung her great head down so that Mia could stroke her in her favourite spot behind her ears.

Mia laughed as Honey sniffed her hands. Honey had been at the centre for six weeks, since her owner couldn't afford to keep her. She was rather greedy, and would do anything for a treat or a pat. It meant that she'd been really good and easy to train – but sometimes it made her a bit naughty, too. Once Mia and Mum had tied her up outside while they were mucking out her stable and she'd nibbled at the quick-release knot to untie herself and gone into Star's stall to eat all her feed. It had taken ages to drag her away!

"Hold on, I'll find you something," Mia said, racing back over to the stables. She went into the feed room where the sacks of chaff, coarse mix, nuts and hay were kept, and found a couple of carrots. Sticking one in her pocket, she carefully broke the other one in half and put it in a bucket, before going back over to the greedy pony.

"Now, don't eat this all at once," she said, holding out the bucket. She giggled as the pony rushed to put her head inside and munched it eagerly.

"Good girl," Mia said, stroking Honey's cheek while she chewed happily, then planting a kiss on her velvety-soft nose.

At that moment, Dapple cantered

over to see what Honey was getting. Mia giggled and held out the bucket to give her a piece of carrot, too. Dapple was a beautiful grey pony, twelve hands high, with dark grey speckles all over her back. She had been at the centre for eight months. When she'd arrived she was so wild that she'd bite and kick at anyone that went near her, but now she was a happy and friendly horse. Her previous owner had ridden her in badly fitting tack that had left sores on her back and made her scared of saddles, so Mum had been determined to find her a home where she wouldn't have to be ridden.

"Mum told me about your new home, Dapple," she said, stroking the grey pony. She would be so sad when Dapple left the centre, but she was pleased that they'd found the perfect place for her. Last night Mum had told her that Dapple was going to a loving home to be a companion pony to a retired racehorse. Mia knew that horses hated being on their own, so it would be great for the racehorse to have a friend, and it was a big family, so there were lots of children to give Dapple plenty of attention. And best of all, nobody would ride her – Dapple was going to love it.

Giving Dapple and Honey one more pat, Mia went to find Mum and Polly. Since Polly was a new arrival, she'd have to stay up in the isolation stables for a while to make sure that she didn't have any germs that she could give the other horses. There were six isolation stalls in total, each with their own small turn-out paddock, so the horses could still go outside even when they weren't allowed to be with the others.

Mia's wellie boots crunched on the gravel as she raced over to the isolation stalls at the very edge of the centre. "Mum? Polly?" Mia called gently as she went towards the stall right at the end of the row. But there was no reply.

At first Mia thought the stables were empty. Usually when she went to see the horses, they put their heads over the stable doors curiously to see who was coming. *I'm sure Mum said she was in the last stall*, Mia thought to herself.

Mia almost walked right up to the stable door before she spotted her. There, cowering in the back corner, was Polly. Her ears were so far back on her head that they were almost invisible and her tail swished from side to side anxiously. She had a brown head with a white snip on her nose. Her mane was light blonde and her eyes were a gorgeous deep chocolatey brown, but they were huge and she was breathing quickly with her nostrils flared. Mia didn't need to know anything about horses to see that Polly was a scared, lonely pony.

"Hi Polly," Mia whispered. "It's OK, you're safe now," she promised.

But Polly just cowered in the corner, looking like the saddest pony in the world.

Collect the whole series...

Based on a real-life animal rescue
RSPCA
Little Lost Hedgehog
Buying this book helps the RSPCA save animals' lives

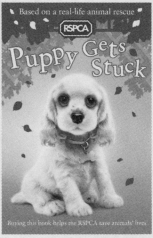
Based on a real-life animal rescue
RSPCA
Puppy Gets Stuck
Buying this book helps the RSPCA save animals' lives

Based on a real-life animal rescue
RSPCA
Lamb All Alone
Buying this book helps the RSPCA save animals' lives

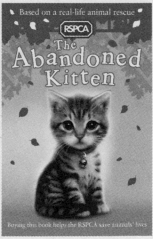
Based on a real-life animal rescue
RSPCA
The Abandoned Kitten
Buying this book helps the RSPCA save animals' lives

Based on a real-life animal rescue

RSPCA

Little Owl Needs a Home

Buying this book helps the RSPCA save animals' lives

Based on a real-life animal rescue

RSPCA

Bunny Needs a Friend

Buying this book helps the RSPCA save animals' lives

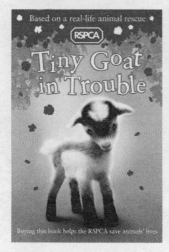

Based on a real-life animal rescue

RSPCA

Tiny Goat in Trouble

Buying this book helps the RSPCA save animals' lives

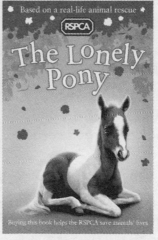

Based on a real-life animal rescue

RSPCA

The Lonely Pony

Buying this book helps the RSPCA save animals' lives

Join the RSPCA!

You'll receive:

- **six issues of *animal action* magazine**
- **a brilliant welcome pack**
- **a FAB joining gift**
- **and a FREE gift with every issue.**

Go to: **www.rspca.org.uk/theclub**

Ask an adult to call:
0300 123 0346 and pay by debit/credit card.

ALL FOR £15!
(£22 OVERSEAS)

RSPCA, Wilberforce Way, Southwater, Horsham, West Sussex RH13 9RS
The RSPCA helps animals in England and Wales. Registered charity no. 219099

DATA ON MINORS IS NEVER DISCLOSED TO THIRD PARTIES AND WE DO NOT SEND DIRECT MARKETING FUNDRAISING
LITERATURE TO UNDER 18S. PLEASE ALLOW 28 DAYS FOR DELIVERY.   AASCH12

For more information on the Animal Action Club check out: www.rspca.org.uk/theden